FINNEGAN
FOR
MAYOR

By
Paula M. Caron
and
Suzi Higley

To Gavin &
Happy Reading!
Suzi Higley-Konopka

FINNEGAN

Finnegan for Mayor
Copyright 2015 by Paula M. Caron and Suzi Higley
Photographs by Suzi Higley

Published by Piscataqua Press
An imprint of RiverRun Bookstore
142 Fleet St.
Portsmouth, NH 03801
www.piscataquapress.com

ISBN: 978-1-939739-61-2

Printed in The United States

Other books by Suzi Higley: *The Adventures of Finnegan Begin*

Dedicated to the Mayors who are running our communities throughout the United States.

Hi, my name is Finnegan and I am a Carolina Dog.

You may be wondering, what is a Carolina Dog?

A Carolina Dog is a Dingo Mix. I am pretty sure I am mixed with Chow, Husky, and Welsh Corgi. I think I may have Beagle in me because when I get the opportunity I love to chase rabbits and turkeys.

I am currently running
for Mayor.

What is a Mayor,
you ask?

A Mayor is the "Top Dog"
in the city!

The Mayor's job is overseeing
the business of the city,
which includes the
Fire Department,
Police Department,
Trash Collection and
Parking Management,
just to name a few.

My friend Phil and I discussing the parking situation!

I have received Phil's endorsement to run for Mayor!

High Five, Phil!

My platform for Mayor is to create more Dog Parks, much like the one on Pierce Island. Why is this such a great dog park, you might ask?

It is a more natural, open space that has great trails. The dogs and their family members can run around the trails and on hot days they can go swimming in the ocean, too!

Hopefully, as Mayor I can get additional funding for more dog parks like this one.

Playing with my friends at the Pierce Island Dog Park.

What a beautiful gift for us to be able
to come and romp around in a natural habitat.

Thank you to all who have helped create this dog park!!!

My brother Burbon is helping me get in shape to run for Mayor.

Enjoying another fun day
at the Dog Park!

And then there are the guys at Joe's Pizza!

I show up on their doorstep and they have a couple of delicious meatballs for me.

Running for Mayor is a lot of work! The guys at Joe's help keep me fueled so I have energy. This allows me to meet the wonderful people and their four-legged friends.

Finnegan
and
the boys!

I would love to work at Joe's Pizza, however those pesky "Board of Health Regulations" don't allow fur around food.

This is another reason I am motivated to run for "Top Dog", Mayor.

As Mayor I am going to change the system from within.

As Mayor, I also want to have a lovely year round central location for indoor and outdoor gardening.

All ages could come and work in this garden; the elders could share their knowledge with the younger.

It would supply jobs and fresh, local food for the community. Us four-legged friends could come and sit awhile.

Year round gardening, how could that be done? With the use of hydroponic growing!

As I enjoy a day on the beach, I ponder my past. I have lived in North Carolina, Vermont and now New Hampshire. I have worn many hats in my life and have met many people.

I have often been told "how cute I am", "how well behaved I am", "how handsome I am", and "how special and kind I am". I have even been told I do not seem like the type to get flustered if something difficult comes up.

I have been a Fashion Model, a Fisherman, and a Hunter. I have had many wonderful friends and taken some amazing road trips, however, these stories I will save for another day.

One of my many fans at
a Meet and Greet

Traveling the countryside
meeting the people.

My brother Burbon, cousin Mazie and I say,
"May the best candidate for Mayor win".

I will tell it to you straight.
I am the only candidate who is going to improve the dog parks in the city.

I will even give you and your families free parking on Sundays.

I will advise all businesses to have large bowls of fresh water outside their doors for us four-legged friends.

I will allow families to bring their dogs into restaurants. After all, dogs are family members - just in different clothing.

I will have year round gardens and a place people of all ages can gather on Saturday nights to mingle and dance.

I love to dance!

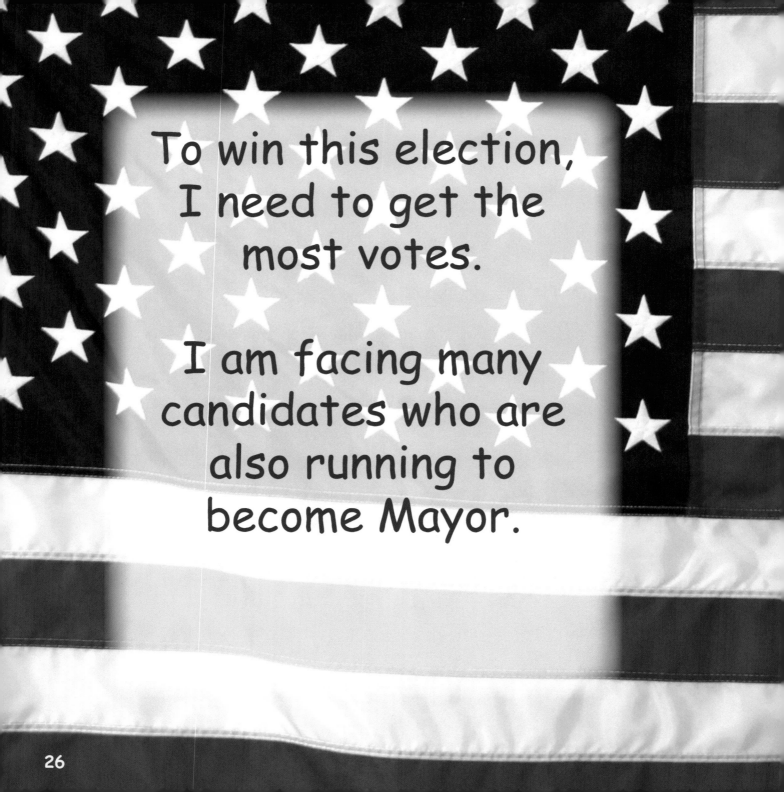

To win this election, I need to get the most votes.

I am facing many candidates who are also running to become Mayor.

Election Day!!

Now that you have read
my book and learned what I,
as Mayor, want to
accomplish...

Will you vote for me?

LIVE FREE and BE HAPPY.

Sincerely, Mr. Finnegan

Finnegan for Mayor!!

Paula M. Caron was born and raised in Beverly, MA. Ms. Caron holds a B.A. Degree in Liberal Arts, from Merrimack College in North Andover, MA. Paula has written extensively about her late Father, Henry "Skeets" Caron's heroic war efforts during WWII. She is the author of "To My Son and Others, Thanks For Serving". This was written while her son served in the Marines.

Paula now resides in Portsmouth, NH.

Suzi Higley was born in Malden, MA and raised in Stratham, New Hampshire. She lived in Jeffersonville, VT for a number of years. While in Vermont she attended Johnson State College and received her B.S. Degree in Health Sciences. She has worked in the Health and Wellness field for over 20 years as a Group Instructor, Personal Trainer and Presenter. She has a love for the outdoors and animals; it is this love of animals that has resulted in helping four-legged friends in need and inspired her to co-write this book, as well as write *The Adventures of Finnegan Begin*.

She resides in Portsmouth, NH.

We hope you enjoy!

CPSIA information can be obtained at www.ICGtesting.com
Printed in the USA
BVIW12n1215120115
382794BV00001B/2